DUKAWALLA
and other stories

ALSO BY PHEROZE NOWROJEE

Pio Gama Pinto: Patriot for Social Justice

A Vote for Kenya: The Elections and the Constitution

A Kenyan Journey

Conserving the Intangible

Cover:

Dukawalla,
ink wash,
Terry Hirst,
1966

DUKAWALLA
and other stories

Pheroze Nowrojee

MANQA
books

NAIROBI

Published by Manqa Books
www.manqa.net

Cover art: *Dukawalla* by Terry Hirst (ink wash, 1966)
Editing by Villoo Nowrojee and Edward Miller
Book design by Edward Miller
Text set in Adobe Garamond Pro

First Edition
10 9 8 7 6 5 4

To

BINAIFER, SIA and ELCHI,
for kindness and love

and

TERRY HIRST (1932–2015),
compass to Kenyan creativity

Thanksgiving

PALI IS a common abbreviation of several names for both our sons and our daughters, and so, over the years that I had known the Deshnath family, it would not have occurred to me to question the name. Pali certainly never sounded unusual. She was their daughter, and I had known them ever since they had arrived in Britain twenty years ago.

They had reached Leicester via Uganda, Idi Amin, and the refugee camps, and, ultimately, through the rehabilitation committees, found the East African community that we were in this Midlands city. Both had been schoolteachers at the time of the expulsion in 1973. On settlement in Leicester, Mr Deshnath had been jobless for a long while and then was fortunate in obtaining a clerical post in the city council. There he had remained till he had been retired. Mrs Deshnath had started in a factory, graduated to a supermarket, moved laterally through several of these, up to a department store, and was now a supervisor in that same department store.

Pali was an only child and much the centre of attention of her parents. I had put it down to the fact that they were older than usual for a child that young, and all such parents are anxious parents. So that now, when Pali was a young lady and beginning to realize the promise she had always shown, her parents were grey and her father was now already in his early seventies.

Their daughter was, as most late children are, quite precocious, and was about to complete her university degree. She was to carry on to postgraduate work, and it was in that connection that she came one day to ask me if I, being in the same field, would be one of her referees. I said of course I would, and she said she would drop by her forms for me to complete and add my letter.

In due course she did, and they lay for a few days unopened while I was out of town. When I returned, I turned to the task and took them to the laboratory to draft my remarks.

Upon going through the application, I was pleasantly surprised to learn that both Mr and

Mrs Deshnath had been professors at a university in India before they had been in Uganda. Moreover, they had taught the same subjects that I had briefly, before I had moved into commercial research. But more than that, I was intrigued reading Pali's name as entered on the form. It suggested the appellation we had known her by for so long, and yet was notably different from others using it.

Pali collected the completed forms from my secretary one afternoon while I was out, and the matter soon passed out of my mind.

I had, however, become interested enough to make it a point to ask the parents more about these aspects of her application.

It was many months later, at a Diwali dinner, that I next saw Mr and Mrs Deshnath. We greeted each other warmly, and they thanked me for having written the reference for Pali. I had by then forgotten the matter, but their effusive gratitude prompted a recall of my curiosity. So I said, 'You know, I wanted to ask you about that.'

Mr Deshnath misunderstood me and said, 'Pali got her admission. She has already started, last month. Thank you so much. I am sure she would not have got into such a prestigious place without your recommendation. She is doing very well. Her supervisors are extremely pleased with her work.'

'I am so glad that she's getting on alright. I would not have expected anything less,' I replied. 'But that is not what I wanted to ask you about. I wanted to ask you about the form.' Mrs Deshnath did not misunderstand me. She replied, 'Yes, she is doing so well. She even wrote to tell us to thank you for all your help. She should be coming home at Christmas and I will remind her to come and thank you.'

So I turned the talk to the fine flavour of our host's food and asked how Mr Deshnath was passing his time these winter days. But as we were parting, I separated him for sufficient time to arrange a meeting the following week at a convenient pub so that I could give him 'some research papers for Pali'.

I almost missed the appointment, immersed in a continuing meeting. When I remembered, I found that the spur generated by Mrs Deshnath's block had evaporated. Then I thought Mr Deshnath would undoubtedly have come, and it would be rude to have made an old person take that trouble on a November evening, not to mention his expectations about some help to Pali in her work.

So I left late, and arrived late, and Mr Deshnath was indeed there, patiently waiting for me. I apologized, handed over the few published papers of mine that I had hastily gathered, and got myself a pint and him a replenishment of his drink. He kept thanking me, even though I kept saying it was nothing and I was glad to be of assistance to Pali at any time, till finally, I said I *did* want to ask him about something. 'Anything, anything,' he replied. 'You are always helping us.'

This of course was not true, and in shame I would even then have hesitated to take advantage of the absence of Mrs Deshnath that I had contrived. But then I thought I would not see them again for some time and that I might as well satisfy my curiosity, having myself travelled so far in the cold. So I said, 'You both were university professors?' 'Oh yes,' he said, 'for many years.' But the casual answer must have recalled something, for his amiable remark had the opposite effect on him, slowly taking away his usual smile. I told him I used to teach the same subjects at the university and was pleased that, even unknowingly, I had shared something with them over all those years. His smile returned, and he said, 'I was taking a quick look at your offprints, and saw that.'

We discussed the titles for a few moments, and then I said, 'And you know, I was also curious about Pali's name, so I wanted to ask you about it.' He kept smiling, silent for a while. 'We never talk about it…but you help Pali so much…'

'Leelavati and I,' he started slowly, 'met while she was in college. I was her professor there. When she graduated—both of us are first class first honours,' he added shyly, 'the university also took her on as a lecturer. So we got married immediately, and continued with our teaching and writing. In time, Leela too became a full professor. We published many papers, and even books. We won several awards. But the thing we most wanted, the honour we most desired, we did not achieve. We could not have a child. Leela went to all the doctors we knew, and to all the doctors we were told about. Then I went. We went to our temple, and to many other temples. We went to churches and fire-temples. We went to astrologers, and some said within five years we would get a child and some said within seven years. One said we would get a child, but not in our country. Others said we should plant certain trees, which we did, or make pilgrimages, which we did. But the five years passed and then the seven years passed, and nothing happened. By that time we had been married fifteen years, and we were slowly trying to be reconciled to this terrible deprivation. I had married late anyway, and soon Leela would not be able to bear a child.

'One day at work when I was glancing at the university appointments pages in a newspaper, something else caught my eye. It said *"Teachers wanted for private secondary school in Uganda"*, for several subjects, interviews to be held, apply, and so on. I then recollected that many years ago one of the astrologers had said that we would have a child, but not in India. I wondered if we could have a child in Uganda? Or in some other country? The thought would not leave me, and by the time I reached home I was in a state of considerable excitement.

'I immediately raised the matter with Leela when she returned from a committee meeting. I spoke at length on the possibilities, but at the end Leela just laughed at me. "These are just fantasies," she said even the next day when I renewed the discussion, and she would not talk about it further. But now the matter began to obsess me and I could not help bringing up the subject constantly.

'As the week drew on, Leela began to point out to me that it was a ridiculous option, that we were university professors and could not consider going to teach in a school, that we were too old to start afresh abroad, that it was nonsense. But both of us knew that my persistent thoughts had nothing to do with careers or titles. I finally wore down Leela to the point where she agreed that I should at least find out more, and soon the post brought us some particulars.

'We did not say it to each other, but we knew that though this was only a chance, it was perhaps the last chance. We had never even thought about that prediction made to us more than ten years ago, nor weighed it in the terms we were now actively considering. Would we come to regret, having tried everything else that was suggested to us, not trying this too, now that the realization was upon us? Had we received a message?

'When we gave in our resignations at the university, we were met with total incredulity. We were reversing everything we had worked for so hard, destroying our achievements, courting poverty, we were possessed, we had lost our reason. We were glad when we had to leave within a very short time.

'We arrived in Kampala and were met and made comfortable by our employer. We began teaching.

'I have to tell you that six months later Leela became pregnant, and the next year Pali was born.

'We were so overcome that for a long while our only thoughts were of taking care of Pali and expressing our unending gratitude. Our families in India were beside themselves. Prayers of thanks went on for months. We sent money to all our temples. We sent money, garlands and *mithai* several times to the young seer whose prediction had so astonishingly come true for us so many years later.

'But our greatest debt, our overwhelming gratitude, was to the country that gave us Pali. We named Pali for the place where she was born. That is the name you saw on the form. Her name is Kampala. To Uganda what could we give in return that could ever repay our debt? We were only teachers. We determined that we would serve it till we died. It was all we could offer. We applied for and became citizens of Uganda.

'And so it was that, when the following November we were all expelled, it was to Britain that we were sent, and then holding only Pali, on to you friends in Leicester.'

Saving Grace

AS HE OPENED his shop in the morning, Natwarlal Khetshi reached out his hand for the usual price tag near the door. It said, '*Unga Sh.1/10.*' He put it under the counter and brought up another one. It read, '*Unga Sh.1/20.*' He put it on the gunny sack from which he had removed the first one, and settled back behind the counter.

The sky was still dark, but below, on the horizon through the few buildings around him, there were light shades of red, and occasional silver, bringing in the new day to the small township below Ol Donyo Sabuk. Natwarlal drew the threadbare shawl tighter around him, as the highland air still kept its pre-dawn chill. Away on the other side, the mountain would become visible with first light and command the long plain to it, till cloud slowly assembled around it and the haze gathered below, and then quickly the peaks would disappear for the rest of the day.

Natwarlal moved in his shop, indifferent to the wonder of the high snows. Nothing happened for half an hour.

Then, the sun now up, the first customers reached him. One of the men among them said, 'How much?' and pointed to the maizemeal sack. Natwarlal got up reluctantly and went around to the bags. He lifted the new sign and said in ungrammatical Swahili that his accent made even more unrecognizable, '*Ona ni shillingi moja na senti shirini.*' There was silence from the man he was addressing and those next to him. 'But,' said Natwarlal, raising his voice, 'since you are the first customer I have had today, I will reduce it for you, and make it one shilling and only ten cents.'

The man lifted a corner of his *shuka* and, untying the knot there, became engrossed in the task of separating out the necessary coins. At last he pushed forward his arm. Natwarlal, his eyes unable to look away, took the coins in a seemingly careless gesture and, the coins sounding, counted them. He found five-cent and ten-cent coins, together totalling fifty-five cents. Without a word, Natwarlal picked up a leaf from his small heap of old newspaper pieces. He lifted a battered tin scoop, measured out a half pound on to the paper and expertly dropped it on to the scale, simultaneously exchanging with his other hand the weight already on the other side for two four-ounce pieces. The scale went up and down, and as it rose again Natwarlal in one flowing motion lifted off the contents, folded the newspaper around the maizemeal, and, pulling on a ball of thin and fragile string next to him, encircled the small bundle several times in swift moves, broke off the string and handed over the package to the man.

As the group moved away Natwarlal leaned down, rose and went around the counter. He lifted off the Sh.1/20 sign, and restored the Sh.1/10 sign to its original place on the sack. Retracing his way, he sank onto his stool behind the counter and sighed.

As the morning wore on, he mechanically served customers. Behind him, a door, lost within the goods displayed on it, hid the rest of the house and the rest of his family.

His shop was made of stone, but that is not

how he had started as a young boy of fourteen. He had first worked in the shops of others, then in corrugated iron sheds of his own, till over the past nearly twenty years, by incrementally accumulating slim heaps of ten-cent and half-shilling coins, he had now, in 1951, put up this stone building in slow instalments. Most of his neighbours were still becalmed in shops that had corrugated iron walls, corrugated iron roofs and corrugated iron doorways. His shop, in addition to being in stone, had small rooms behind it on each side, enclosing a courtyard. Only the rear was a wall of corrugated iron sheets cross-beamed into a tall gate.

A free-standing tap and shiny cooking vessels decorated the attempted enclave. Occasionally, the problems of the courtyard would impinge upon the front of the shop. Voices would rise in shrill incoherence. Or a child's insistent crying would not stop. Natwarlal would rudely push these interruptions back, and his wife had learnt not to let matters drain over from her side of the house to his.

As lunch approached he rose to close the shop.

His wife looked around the door. 'Food is ready. Are you coming?' Not bothering to answer, he put on his faded black coat. Seeing this, she in turn did not bother to wait for a further reply. Natwarlal went out from the rear and entered the back street between the buildings. A gutter ran down each side. When he reached the broader street, he turned towards the government offices. Passing these he walked on till he came to his destination.

He entered the Sikh Gurdwara. The small room that was the temple lay in front of him, but he went to a side, to where benches and tables flanked it. A few persons were already eating the lunch that the *langar* provided. Natwarlal went to the small counter at the kitchen window. There he was served with a full *thali*. One of the regular volunteers greeted him, '*Sat Sri Akal*, Natwar Sahib.' He said nothing and continued eating. 'So what have you been doing today?' Another one answered, 'Making money.' Everyone sniggered. A stranger walked in hesitantly. Someone got up and directed him to the kitchen window. The first speaker said to no one in particular, 'That is what this place is for.' Then facing Natwarlal he said, 'Are you a traveller, Natwar Sahib?' One of the others shouted raucously from the end of the shed that served as the dining area, 'Yes, he travels here every day from his shop. He is a traveller.' A voice rose, 'So is that why he has to eat in this Gurdwara every day?' Natwarlal looked up. 'I have to respect God,' he muttered. There was short derisive laughter. When he had finished, Natwarlal left.

In the evening, his wife managed the winding down of the movement in the house. The five children with them ate their meal at sunset with Natwarlal. She cleared up after them, and then ate her own meal. By now the house was in darkness. There were never lights in the house. Only one kerosene lamp was used, and for only one purpose. Presently it lay unlit in a corner. As he, his wife and four of the children readied for bed, Natwarlal called for the lamp. He took it from his eldest daughter, shook it and tested the level of the kerosene, always to be kept at no more than just needed. He lit it and carefully adjusted the wick down till he was satisfied. He then handed it to the girl. This was the one in her last year in middle school, who at the end of this year would be sitting her qualifying examination for secondary school. The girl headed with it to the shop area, for she studied there each night at the big counter. As she reached the door, Natwarlal called her back. 'Give me the lamp,' he said, and then, 'I have a letter from Rakesh.' His wife looked up.

He opened the envelope and began reading to her slowly the closely handwritten pages from their eldest child. The back of the discarded envelope read: '*From Rakesh Khetshi, Houghton Hall, London School of Economics, London.*'

Masterji

WE ALL LIVED together in the colony, but we had little knowledge of each other. Looking at us as we all moved busily on the city's well-kept streets, an onlooker would have thought the contrary and gained the impression that we also shared much else. In fact, we did not share basic social or economic experiences. Even the range of streets, of which we were temporary joint tenants during the day, was limited. When the day ended, the roads leading out of the city were not the same corridors of passage for all. We went to different destinations. These were not roads to each other, they were the boundaries between us. Some people would not care to use them to us. And any use by us to move to them would have been viewed by them as trespass. There was no fence, but in between there was the deep trench of colour. If you stood at a particular vantage point, the trench might not be visible, and some people therefore said that really there was no barrier. We met in the workplace, and some thought therefore that they knew the people working around them. But when we left the office, we took those different roads and went into houses the others never entered, and they into houses we never entered. So we knew nothing of how those others lived. Or they about how we lived. Or how we died.

And in this latter gap, one man survived to live another life.

My story opens in 1990 outside a supermarket in North London, which my elderly teacher and friend, Mr Mehra, and his wife were about to enter. A middle-aged man coming towards them suddenly cried out and fell at Mr Mehra's feet. Clasping them, he kept saying, 'Masterji, Masterji.'

Mr and Mrs Mehra were startled, but stood still at this peaceful, even respectful, assault. Mr Mehra looked at the man steadily in the same way he had viewed thousands in the classroom all those many years ago, for Mr Mehra was now in his mid-eighties. After some questing moments

looking down, Mr Mehra at last said in a kindly
voice, 'Madan, get up. Get up.'

The man, whom no one had called that for
a very long time, stood up. His palms held together in front of him in inexpressible respect, he
remained before Mr Mehra, his eyes cast down.
'Come, come,' said Mr Mehra, smiling. 'Let us go
where we can talk. We live just round the corner.
Come.'

'How are you? What have you been doing all
these years?' Mr Mehra asked as they walked. But
the man kept silent, simply holding on to Mr
Mehra's hand till they reached the house. It had
not been dissimilar thirty-three years ago.

*

Those many years ago, a distraught figure
knocked repeatedly on the door of Mr Mehra's
modest house on Desai Road in Nairobi late
one evening. Mr Mehra lived near the school.
Mrs Mehra called him; he was marking the day's
submitted exercise books.

He looked at the dishevelled young man before

him for a second before noting that it was Madan Sohal, one of his old boys, who in his last year in school had been one of his favourite prefects. He had passed out about five years ago. 'What is it?' Mr Mehra asked.

'Sir, help me, sir, help me,' the young man cried out, moving restlessly on his feet, unable to keep still.

'Sir, help me,' he said, clutching at Mr Mehra's hands.

When he was brought in and made to sit, the story came out. The police were after him. They had arrested others, Madan's three friends. The four boys—for to Mr Mehra they remained eternally his 'boys', though these were reckless and irresponsible twenty-plus-year-olds now—were long out of school and earning a living, and sometimes not earning it.

They had bought stolen car parts and then had sold them to one of the bazaar shopkeepers. Those parts had turned out not to be in working order. The irate buyer had come home and demanded his money. Time had passed, and they had still not been able to return his money, nor recover their own. The man had gone to the police. There had been inquiries and statements, but the day's arrests were preludes to charges being laid in court the next morning, and Madan did not know what to do.

After many questions, and several not wholly satisfactory answers, Mr Mehra advised that Madan should appear in court the next morning without waiting to be arrested, and said that he would ask one of the lawyers, an ex-student of his, to assist. A telephone call was made, and the lawyer confirmed that he would be present in court and represent Madan.

The next day the boys' pleas were taken and the hearing date was set. They were released on a cash bail, which amount, though not very big, was a serious burden on Madan's family. The father had died when Madan and his two sisters were small, and they had since lived with his uncle, in unsatisfactory dependence, in a family neither extended nor nuclear.

The case came on for mentions and then

several times for hearing, but never took off, and the matter dragged on for several months. The pressures of inactivity and the disqualification from even casual jobs, for the bazaar man made sure no one employed these four young men, took its toll on Madan. As the months passed, things at home steadily deteriorated into ever more problems. When a Kampala trader offered Madan some part-time work driving lorries from Nairobi, Madan was glad for it. He kept returning in time for mentions and hearings, but the case did not move.

In Kampala, away from the family, Madan had had time to reflect on his problems. He could not see any way out. His lawyer had not seen much of a defence. He faced charges of obtaining by false pretences, worse, of receiving stolen property, and the lawyer had advised him of the prejudice in the courts against that offence. In fact, at their last meeting he had asked Madan to consider whether he wanted to plead guilty and try for leniency. His co-accused were not helping in any way. Every alternative he could imagine seemed to end only in his being sent to prison. The thought had petrified him: not out of fear for himself, but for what it would do to those in the house. And now in a few days' time he would have to return to Nairobi, and this time the hearing would certainly go on. At the last mention, the magistrate had deprecated all the delay and insisted that he himself would commence the hearing *and* complete it the next time, without further adjournment.

As the days passed, panic invaded Madan. Every hour seemed to ensure more and more certainly the prospect of jail. The nights screamed inevitability. Madan was paralysed.

*

The call was from Kampala.

'Is that Mr Mehra?'

'Yes.'

'I am calling from Kampala. My name is Harpinder Singh.'

'Yes?'

'I am a friend of Madan Sohal. He worked with us. He always told me to speak to you if anything was needed in Nairobi.'

'Yes?'

'He has died.'

Mr Mehra remained silent.

'This is terrible,' he said at last. 'What happened?'

'There was a motor car accident, sir.'

'When?'

'Yesterday. We are sending his body back to Nairobi. For the funeral. So that he can be cremated there. He used to say that you always helped his family.'

Mr Mehra, with his eldest son Bhagoo, was at Madan's house early next morning when the body arrived in a pickup from Kampala. Police constables were in attendance, for when he had failed to turn up in court the police had gone to his house. They had been informed of the accident, and had now returned to witness the arrival of the corpse.

Mr Mehra had arranged with the pandit from the Arya Samaj that the prayers would be held at home at one o'clock, and the cremation would take place at two in the afternoon. He informed the police of these arrangements, and they had left saying they would return for the cremation.

The body was placed in the front room of the cramped two-room dwelling, the family praying intermittently. Everyone deferred to Mr Mehra, elder of the community. Mr Mehra stood aside with Bhagoo, talking occasionally in low tones. Before he left to make further arrangements for the hearse, he thought he should pay his last respects to his pupil. In a quiet moment when the room was empty, he stepped forward with Bhagoo and gently undid the winding sheet around the face and moved it aside.

The darker features of an unknown Ugandan, peaceable in death, looked back at him.

Mr Mehra fell back in shock and comprehension. At that moment, an old lady entered the room, saw the exposed face, and saw Mr Mehra. Mr Mehra and the old lady looked at each other for a long moment. Then she fell at his feet and held him around the legs. Her body shook with long soundless sobs of fear. After what seemed like eons of danger and certain discovery, Mr Mehra's hand moved slowly and found the cloth. Covering the face again, he carefully pinned the sheet back so it could not be opened easily. Then lifted the old lady up and sat her down on the nearby chair. He turned and left. Bhagoo, a silent witness to all that had happened, followed him.

*

Mr Mehra had only a few years to retirement. His had been a long career that had been marked by industry and integrity, rather than any unusual intellect. With these, he had overcome the numerous and nasty barriers inherent in the colonial system to become an Education Officer, and often the Acting Headmaster of this secondary school. The Education Department had sent him on several overseas courses, and to many conferences. He would, in a short time, be ending his career, with the respect of all. Was that to be put at risk? He had worked his whole adult life, ever since he left the Teacher Training College. He had supported his family and, later, his widowed sisters, and brought up his nephews and nieces in addition to his own children. He was held in the highest regard in the community and by his government superiors. Was all that to be wiped out at a stroke just for this one errant lad? Should he not retire with honour?

But the boy was his student. It was a strange bond that tied these children to him for life. What if they had become men? What if they had breached what society laid down? Worse, forgotten all that he had taught them? Forgotten all that he had not known how to teach them, but had nevertheless hoped they had learnt anyway? Now when he was at the point of ending his own long endeavours, become all that he had ever wanted to be, should he not protect what he had worked so hard for? But could he turn his back on one of his own students? Could any teacher turn away from a call for help from any one of his students? Would he be able to live with that?

What would happen to Madan's mother, the old lady who had fallen at his feet? Could the family come to the temple again? Where would they look when looked at? How would they live?

He was not even sure how many children Madan and his very young wife had. Two? Or only one? He had not noticed.

He could turn to nobody to help him in this decision. Bhagoo was his son, his companion, an extension of himself. Bhagoo had already started working in a bank, a job obtained with effort. He had to think of what Bhagoo's employers might do, even though Bhagoo was ready to help, even though he was as discreet as Mr Mehra himself. Bhagoo should not be asked to make such a decision. Sharing the burden with anyone else would endanger the boy in Kampala, perhaps betray him. This was something he would have to decide by himself. Would he be able to live with what Madan was now asking of him?

'He told me to speak to you if anything was needed.' But this? And even if he thought Madan should turn to him, could he himself be the instrument of assistance? Would that not be irresponsible of him, letting down his own family and the whole community? This would be aiding and abetting a crime, this would get him taken to court and into the shaming pages of the newspapers. His name would be on air, on the bulletins of the Hindustani Service of the Kenya Broadcasting Service, indelibly staining his family. This could not be hushed up by the figures of influence he knew, his superiors in the department who thought so highly of him. Nor by any quiet word they could whisper. He would be made an example of, and the whole community taught a lesson.

*

'Open the sheet,' said Inspector Whitley brusquely. He had arrived at the crematorium just as they were about to light the pyre. The body had been laid among the large sandalwood pieces, the sheet having been secured back tightly underneath.

'No, no,' said Bhagoo. 'That would not be holy.'

'Open it,' Whitley barked.

'No, no, these people cannot show their face. It is not done in his tradition.'

'I have attended other cremations,' said the Inspector. 'I have seen other faces. *Chalo, chalo,* open the sheet.'

Inspector Whitley fancied himself on his knowledge of the Indian world in Nairobi, particularly its underworld, and used the Hindi words to signal that.

'No, no. These people are different. Once they are wrapped in this cloth of their religion, and prayers are over, they cannot open it again.'

Bhagoo's obvious sincerity made the Inspector hesitate. He did not want to leave anything un-checked before closing the Police file and the case in court next week. He had also been angry that this insolent youth had escaped punishment. At the same time, he did not want to show disrespect or disrupt the ceremony in front of the few seri-ous old men and the weeping mother and wife of the deceased. They were unusually present and visibly in tears and great grief. Nor did he want to have to explain to the Commissioner why he had violated and injured religious and communal feelings, something the Government was always careful to avoid doing—more so at this time when the Emergency looked like it was winding down and the Police needed support and information from the community on a daily basis.

The Inspector held back the hand he had extended to pull off the sheet himself. 'Who are *they?*'

'These people? Him, you mean? I mean... these people are...from there,' answered Bhagoo, pointing in the direction of the ocean hundreds of miles away. 'They are very sacred. More than us. More than Arya Samaj. They are...Uttam Samaj people, very sacred,' said Bhagoo.

The Inspector had never heard of 'Uttam Samaj', though, of course, he knew of the Arya Samaj, and had heard vaguely of the Brahma Samaj. But these people and their bloody religious groups proliferated every second week, and he was not going to start investigating some new upstart church here, on a Saturday afternoon, when he was about to go to the Wanderers ground for the match. 'Well, he wasn't very "sacred",' the Inspector sneered. 'Bloody thief.' And got up.

34

The pandit poured more ghee around the body. The eldest boy being a child, an aged family member lit the pyre. Bhagoo stood to a side. Mr Mehra stood behind him. They left after the ashes had been collected and handed over to Madan's uncle.

*

They entered the North London house. 'I hope, Madan,' said Mr Mehra, eternally the school-teacher, 'that you have been behaving yourself here.'

Close to the Mahatma

IN THE CHILL dark of the Highlands, small groups stood on the cleared ground that served as the station platform. Mist moved about. It was long past midnight. In the approaching train, a man was still reading a book. As it neared Lumbwa on the Western Rift, the train slowed unexpectedly, for it was not a scheduled stop. The man stood up and, lowering a window, looked out.

His name was Charlie Andrews. In 1904, the Reverend Charles F. Andrews had come out to India from Britain as a Missionary. After spending time at Delhi University, he joined Tagore at Shantiniketan. Then, at the request of Prof. Gokhale, he had gone to South Africa to see Gandhi and *satyagraha* at work. There in the Mahatma's South African struggles had been forged a close and lasting bond between them. After Gandhi left South Africa, their work continued in India, together in the struggle against the British. And now, in 1920, this trusted friend of Gandhi was in Kenya, at the direction of the Mahatma, to report on the discriminatory treatment of the Indians here, and more importantly, on the intense political push by the colonial settlers for White Self-rule and racial supremacy in Kenya.

Ahead he saw a few lanterns along the line of the train. Over the grating metal of the brakes bringing the train to a hissing halt, he heard voices in the dark. Some were calling, 'Here, here.' From the other end, fainter voices also said, 'Here, here.' Yet others said, 'No, no. Here.' He heard sounds of people slipping on the high ballast around the sleepers, and stumbling as they ran in the darkness, unsure of where to find him. The women called out anxiously to the children, 'Where are you going? Come back here.'

When at last it was discovered which window he was at, an irregular semicircle of the lanterns materialized below his compartment. They recalled for him simple Diwali lamps in a small town. The ladies, clad in sarees and meekness, stood at the edges, holding garlands of flowers in their hands. Several people spoke at once. A small boy kept calling out, 'Mr Andrew, Mr Andrew, Mr Andrew.' One of the mothers stepped forward shyly and said, '*Namaste.*' Andrews joined his palms in response, and bowed his head quickly. A bigger boy in a school uniform with a tie and blazer kept raising his hand up, offering something to Andrews. Andrews leaned down and took the object and held it up to the compartment light. It was a one shilling coin. Andrews leaned down again and said, 'I will give it to Bapu. It will be put to good use. Thank you, thank you.'

Different voices sought to engage him, till someone hushed them. Mr Barot cleared his throat. In the silence of the dark, it sounded unduly loud. He was about to make a speech. Mr Barot was the senior clerk in the High Court at Kisumu. On receiving his instructions from Congress earlier in the day, he had rushed over to Lumbwa. On his way, he had thought back to the speech of the Chief Justice when the latter had opened the Criminal Appeal Sessions earlier that year, and Mr Barot tried to incorporate as much of it as he could in his speech. The Stationmaster whispered, 'Quickly, quickly. The train must go.'

Mr Barot looked disdainfully at this

insignificant official, who, unlike him, was not among those who habitually were near the Chief Justice and the Puisne Judges. Assuming his deeper voice, he started: 'Distinguished Revered Andrews, we thank the Almighty for return of peace. We are thanking you also for all efforts for freedom that you are making for us. We condemn bad behaviour to you by certain persons in Nakuru. We know you have been treated in hospital by doctors. But that has not stopped you, you are still helping us. You are good man. [There were murmurs of approval.] We know you have been berated and beaten for working for Mahatma Gandhi and for our freedom. God Save the King.' He stopped abruptly. 'My youngest daughter will now present you with our flowers.' He held up the small girl to the carriage window, while the ladies with the garlands stepped forward and gave them to the girl who stretched and handed them over one by one to Andrews. Andrews was deeply moved. He was very familiar with their significance, and with awkward movements placed them around his own neck. A few people clapped. He kept repeating, 'Thank you, thank you.'

The Stationmaster shifted uneasily from one foot to the other. He would have to explain the halt in the night and the consequent delay, and wanted it as short as possible. The passenger train did not normally stop at Lumbwa. But, in the evening, he had received a call on the railway telephone, and the Stationmaster, Nakuru, had begun speaking to him in an urgent voice. Quite improperly, the instructions had been given only in Punjabi. After he had received the instructions, unsupported by any official telegraph memoranda, he had understood the situation, and knew that Driver Bishen Singh Bedi on the passenger train that night was also in the know. He had willingly agreed, but he felt the shorter the time it took, the better the agreed explanations would hold.

Two days ago, shocking news had reached the Indian community throughout the colony. The Reverend Charles Andrews, the messenger of Mahatma Gandhi, his trusted friend, a freedom fighter known throughout India, who was visiting to report on the situation of the Indians in Kenya, had reached Nakuru. There, he had been dragged out of his train compartment and been kicked and beaten by a gang of young British settlers. Andrews had been taken to hospital and had been treated by doctors.

There was satisfaction when the community learnt that, in London, the Secretary of State for the Colonies, then Mr Winston Churchill, had expressed his view that the offenders should have received the punishment they deserved. But the Reverend Andrews had declined to press charges. The community agreed that that only showed how worthy the Reverend was to be the representative of the Mahatma.

This deeply offending conduct and attack had constituted great disrespect to the Mahatma. Having also been aimed at the community itself, it had angered everyone. Quick consultations had flowed between the East African Indian National Congress offices in Nairobi, Nakuru, Kisumu and other centres. It had become necessary for the community to show its condemnation of this display of white supremacy. It would also be a show of support for the Reverend Charles Andrews' visit and for his continuing work for the Indians in the Empire. A decision had been taken.

That night, Lumbwa had been made the first unscheduled halt, and Mr Barot's group the first to show their appreciation. At the next station, the train was again halted, and Reverend Andrews again honoured. Pandit Rawal had prayed for him, and a trio of schoolgirls had sung a short *bhajan*. The Pandit had then given him some *prasad*. When Andrews had thanked them in his imperfect Hindustani, their faces had lit up, bringing light in the darkness.

At dawn at Kibos, the Chairman of the Sikh Sabha had offered the protective services of four fierce-looking young men carrying swords. Andrews had declined their offer with profuse thanks, telling them Mahatma Gandhi would prefer a nonviolent response to the Nakuru outrage.

The train had finally pulled in at Kisumu Station an hour late. Letters full of indignant complaints from the night's European passengers in the First Class carriages had followed. Their pages were full of the unwarranted delay, the un-acceptable noise, the uncivilized music, and most of all, their unmitigated contempt for unhygienic people who did not know how to behave. But the displeased Railway Administration in Nairobi had also not relished the idea of receiving complaints from Indian religious bodies about the illegality of Railway officials breaking up religious ceremonies, real or pretended, for the Mahatma's emissary.

Nor was the prospect of attacks on Andrews on the way back, and a repeat by the staff of their peaceful but unwelcome remonstrance through more delays, any the more attractive. Accordingly, a discreet phone call had been made to the Commissioner of Police, and on his return journey the following week, Andrews had been provided with police protection while on the train.

At Lumbwa, when the train moved away into the darkness, and the diminishing red rear light on the guard's van had finally dissolved into the night, the groups had turned away and walked out slowly, talking quietly. One of the men whispered, 'Do you know even the Mahatma was thrown out of a train in South Africa and beaten for fighting for freedom? Now his friend has suffered in the same way.' His companion replied, 'It is God's sign.'

That night remained with them through their lives. Mr Barot had proudly reported to M. A. Desai, the Secretary of the East African Indian National Congress, that their *satyagraha* of non-cooperation and delay had annoyed the whites greatly, and had been a great success. Neither the Reverend Andrews' words, nor the impulse to freedom that had made him part with his meagre saving, ever left the student. The young women were often asked by their own children to tell them the story of that night.

Many, many years later, when the news had reached Kenya of Gandhi's assassination, all had thought of that night and how they had become part of the struggle and had become too, so close to the Mahatma.

The Committee Meeting

THE COMMITTEE was convening at eight thirty in the morning. Mr Swaran, the committee member from the staff side, was present outside the Secretariat Boardroom by eight twenty. He was the first to arrive, and the only one for a while. At eight twenty-eight promptly, the Chairman, Mr Orme-Bowyer, and the Committee Secretary, Mr Barrow, arrived. And from the opposite end of the corridor, the other two members headed towards the Boardroom. Mr Swaran constantly admired the effortless punctuality of the English officials. For him, to be punctual he had to be early. But he was trying his best to make it come naturally, for from his wide knowledge of England and English ways he was keenly aware of the high regard in which punctuality and punctual people were held by the English.

The Chairman called the meeting to order. It was an interdepartmental committee to interview some suitable candidates for very minor posts in the Judicial Department. The official term was Subordinate Staff, and indeed they were.

'Let's have the first one,' said the Chairman, and Barrow went out to bring in the candidate. It was a nervous young man in a suit obviously borrowed. Nairobi's climate at that hour is cool throughout the year, but the young man was already sweating visibly.

Barrow turned over his file and spoke for the benefit of all the committee. 'This is Mr Suryadutt Dosaj. He has applied for the post of Punjabi Interpreter in the Resident Magistrate's Court.'

'Sit down, Mr Dosaj,' said the member on the Chairman's right, the one who usually acted as the Deputy in the Chairman's absence. He pointed to the chair arranged so that it faced the committee. 'What languages can you translate from?'

There was a short interval before the young man cleared his throat, found his voice, and commenced in a scratchy whisper. Only the last words reached the committee. '...Punjabi, sir.'

'What languages do you know?' a member asked.

'Punjabi, sir, English, sir, Urdu, sir.'

'And which languages do you think you are good at?'

'Punjabi and English, sir.'

'What languages did you study at school?'

'English, sir, and Urdu.'

So far Dosaj's contribution had consisted only of repeating the names of languages. He had not uttered a single complete sentence, a fact that was not lost on the committee. Barrow leaned over and said, 'Mr Dosaj, take this book. Do you see the passage that is underlined. Please read it for us.'

Dosaj recoiled reflexively. In his short experience, the printed page in a bound volume had always been an object of danger, which year after year he had tried to avoid, a problem that had only been solved by his ejection from the educational process by the passage of years. The dread rushed back, his face flushed.

He girded himself. He stared hard at the short paragraph. Finally he started, hesitatingly.

'*He had spent years on the farm, the vast acres next to Lake Elmenteita, and now he was dying.*

He had built a country. He had spent his fortune bringing seed, and grade cattle and dreams to this faraway place.'

Mr Swaran sucked in his breath loudly. It was a signal to his committee colleagues that he had immediately recognized the passage.

Dosaj continued slowly, stopping at the wrong places and losing all meaning in the effort.

'Now as he lay dying he was not sure whether he had done the best thing for the Home Country.'

At length he petered out, the closing word under his breath, and leaned back wholly exhausted by his exertions. He looked up with frightened eyes at the Chairman.

But it was Barrow who spoke, 'Can you translate the first line into Punjabi?'

The young man looked back at him incredulously. What would this man understand even if I did translate it, he thought to himself in Punjabi.

There was a silence. Barrow said, 'Go on.'

Dosaj shyly broke into Punjabi, unused to ever speaking the language in front of English people. As he completed the requirement, Barrow turned to the Chairman, 'It's passable.' Barrow had come to Kenya from service in the Army in India, and spoke Urdu and Punjabi fluently.

Mr Swaran addressed the applicant. 'You see, this is from the life of Lord Delamere. It is written by Mrs Elspeth Huxley, a lady from our Colony. She comes from a very good family, and she has married into another very, very good family, and very learned. They are Huxleys and Wedgwoods and Darwins themselves.'

The young man stared back in total incomprehension. A few of the panel shifted uncomfortably in their seats. There was complete silence. Then the Deputy, taken aback a little, and who normally would have asked each member if he wanted to ask any questions, simply turned to Barrow and said, 'Let's have the next one.'

Dosaj was led out and Barrow returned with the second interviewee.

'Well, Mr...' and the Deputy looked again at his file papers, 'Upaya...er...'

The young man remained silent. He was resigned to the notion that his name was unpronounceable by any English person, and that it was his fault to possess and offer them such a name.

'…yes, well, why do you want to work in the Courts?'

The young man looked surprised. His father worked in the Law Courts, his uncle worked there, they had always worked there, and he thought everybody knew that when he was eighteen he too would join them and work there. He thought it out.

'My father works in the Courts. My uncle also works in the Courts.'

'What does your father do there?'

The young man answered him more assuredly this time, and proudly. 'He is the clerk of the Poosney Judge in the Supreme Court of…'

Before the Deputy could respond, Mr Swaran leaned forward in his seat, and said to Upadhayaya in a kindly voice. 'Young man, do not say "poosney".' He laughed. 'You must say "pu-ny", puny.' Mr Swaran turned to look at his fellow committee members and smiled at them. There were, the smile said, a few of his sort who did know about these matters. When they looked back at him their eyes were unsmiling, but Mr Swaran did not notice that. He had already turned back to the young man, and was continuing, 'That is because the puisne judge is a small judge, and the Chief Justice is the most important judge. That is why he is the Chief, and the other judge is a puisne judge.'

The other panel members looked away from Mr Swaran. Nobody spoke for a while.

Then one of the members leaned over to the Chairman and said quietly, 'This is Upadhayaya's son. I know the family. He's alright.'

Barrow got up and led the young man out, and returned with the next applicant.

'What is your name, young man?' asked the Deputy.

'Harish Vadalya, sir.'

'And what will you be able to translate?'

'Gujarati speeches, sir.'

'Into English?'

'Yes, sir.'

'Well, here is an English "speech". Let us hear you read it first.'

This young man was more confident, and took the cyclostyled sheet that had been handed to him with greater assurance.

He started carefully, but slowly spoke more evenly. '*Let us therefore* [a hesitation] *brace ourselves to our duties and so bear ourselves that, if the British Empire and its Commonwealth last for a thousand years, men will still say,*' another hesitation, and then he ended, '"*This was their finest hour.*"'

'Good,' said the Deputy. 'Do you know what it means?'

The young man kept quiet. After a while he looked down.

Mr Swaran's voice rose, 'You do not know? He saved you from terrible things and you do not know?'

Mr Swaran looked up at the ceiling. In a high tenor voice he began, '"*We shall fight them on the beaches, we shall fight them on the landing grounds. We shall fight them in the hills, we shall fight them in the streets. We shall never surrender.*"' He drew a breath so as to launch into Winston's next lines.

The Deputy spoke quickly into the pause. 'And can you translate the first line of what you have read?'

Vadalya looked down at the page, and then slowly put together a Gujarati translation.

The Deputy looked on either side of the table

and said, 'Any questions?' The other members looked down in answer, and before Mr Swaran could respond Barrow got up and led Vadalya away.

He returned with a short figure with an over-abundance of hair, not the type one would expect would contribute sobriety to a court. But the eyes were lively and the Deputy said, 'What rank did you usually get in your class?'

The accurate assessment hit its mark, and the young man smiled. 'I was always fifth, sir.' The Deputy smiled back.

'What was your best subject?'

'History and Geography, sir.'

'Would you know something about Sir Francis Drake?'

'Yes, sir. He was sailing around the world.'

The Deputy, who had spent the last three decades also sailing around the world in his various postings, liked the description. 'Who was his Queen?'

The young man thought and said, 'Queen Elizabeth, the Virgin Queen.'

'Do you know what else Sir Francis Drake is famous for?'

But the young man had reached the end of his achievement, or he would not have been in line for this job.

Mr Swaran broke in. 'Do you not remember that he played at bowls while the Spanish Armada was sailing towards England? And when they told him about the danger, he said he would finish his game first?'

The young man nodded uncertainly.

'And do you not remember the other courtiers at Queen Elizabeth's court? Like Sir Walter Raleigh, who covered a puddle with his cloak so Queen Elizabeth could walk over it?' He looked at the young man piercingly, and continued, 'And Sir Philip Sidney? Did he not write sonnets?'

One of the heads near Swaran rose up sharply, but no one said anything.

'Well, yes,' said the Deputy to the young man. 'I think that is about all.'

The young man got up and walked out.

The Chairman leaned to his right and conferred in whispers with his Deputy. Then he leaned to his left and had a brief word with the members there. Then he turned to his right again and looked past the Deputy to Mr Swaran. Mr Swaran smiled back in satisfaction of having conducted himself in a manner befitting a member of such an important Secretariat committee. Mr Swaran was an avid reader and knew much about the English, save, because it was in no book, that if there was someone they despised more than a colonized subject who knew nothing about the glories of England, the English language and English history, it was one who did. So Mr Swaran did not notice that the Chairman did not then consult with him, and instead turned away to speak again to Barrow.

The Chairman stood up. The committee rose with the brush of chairs. He moved towards the door with Barrow. When they reached the doorway he said, 'We'll take all four.' Then he jerked his head over his shoulder at Mr Swaran behind them, and lowered his voice. 'Get rid of him,' he said with quiet venom.

Gift Taken Back

OVER THE PAST two centuries in the Diaspora, without any worldly success or wealth or influence, with nothing other than their quality of warmth and industry, the millions who took off from the Subcontinent became a gift to the faraway countries that had become their new homes.

My friend's father was one of these. But it is unnatural to give away one's children. So the Subcontinent silently retained a prerogative of recall. Only very occasionally has she exercised this cruel right. The case of my childhood friend is one of these.

My friend Rus's father had lost his parents very early, and had grown up in an orphanage into a vital young man, handsome, jovial and with the unforced ability to make instant friends with all he met. Without any family or other social ties to offer alternatives, the prospect of going to

'Africa' was not a search for employment, but an adventure. So, while still in his late teens, he landed in Mombasa joyously ready to take on a new country and any new work.

His energetic charm soon found him a job, and later a small and growing business of his own.

In due course he returned to India to bring a bride, and Rus, their eldest child, was born in Mombasa the year before the Second World War broke out. He was followed over the next fifteen years by a succession of brothers. Rus was a year older than I was, and we first met when I was taken down to Mombasa on my father's local leave to stay at Rus's place.

Unexpectedly, we near-ten-year-olds became instant friends, and then shared all waking moments: in the house, outside a sailors' bar (expressly forbidden to us), out on the main road (likewise strictly forbidden), in their stationary car in the garden 'driving' (allowed). So when the week came to an end all too quickly, it was not surprising that when Rus's father brought home a jacket which Rus had much wanted, he also brought one for me. These were jackets, in a brown corduroy, copying for children the then fashionable leather flying jacket of the recently ended War. My last day there, we wore them constantly and together, as if we were twins dressed up identically by an indulgent, lazy mother. And we duly harvested many questions about us being exactly that. On the train returning upcountry, I remained inseparable from the jacket.

Many months later, in the new year, Rus's father had work in Nairobi and brought Rus up with him. Of course, he showed up wearing the jacket, and I immediately donned mine. By this time my cousins too had similar jackets, and for those two days we all went around together, a similarly dressed quartet.

That same year I travelled to India for schooling. I was to be enrolled at a boarding school in the Western Ghats. Imagine our mutual surprise when at the school I found Rus already a student there. We thought it only natural that I, who had come in the middle of the year and was in a different class, was put in the same school house as Rus. Indeed our jackets did come out, but there being strict uniform at most times, we could only flash them for a few Sundays before our limited attention spans moved on.

We spent the next four years at the school. We were a part of the daily classes, the daily meals, and the daily games that changed with the seasons, the hot cricket season giving way to the football of the muddy monsoon months. We were part of the plays on Parents' Day, although *our* parents were three thousand miles away. We were no great correspondents with them beyond the minimum, reluctant and uninformative efforts of the mandatory letter-writing period, and the only news I remember from his family is that of the birth every couple of years of that line of boys.

When I had finished my school-leaving public examinations, I returned to Nairobi to await the results. When I went down briefly to Mombasa, I was taken over by Rus's parents. His mother, Mrs Dhondy, was an extraordinarily good cook, and I was made to recite my favourite dishes, and then add some, so that nothing less than all of them simultaneously could be fed to me, because I was Rus's best friend. Having such plates in my hand,

I had to be seated and to tell them about Rus. And I was glad to. Rus was doing very well.

I did not see Rus for a year, till another fortuitous convergence of our ways took place. Both of us being foreign students, without homes in Bombay, and now both being enrolled in colleges there, quite independently we turned up one wet June morning at the same communal students' hostel. And so, again, we spent another three years together in another institution.

By now, from many small things and those long years, we were something more than friends, closer than brothers.

In the next two years as Rus was moving to his final year, his increasing achievements in the university cadet corps was making it clear that he was looking at the armed forces after graduation. I left India for home the year before that, but as I was leaving, Rus gave me the news that after six boys and many more years, Mrs Dhondy had finally had the daughter she had always wanted.

At Mombasa, Mr Dhondy collected me from the docks, still as full of energy and good-looks as his son, their only difference Rus's impressive height. I spent the time at their home bringing them up to date on Rus. I went around the next day with Mr Dhondy about his business, where he introduced me to all we met as Rus's friend and his own son too, proud, he would tell them, of what I would be doing in the future.

I never saw Rus again, but in the coming years I saw a fair amount of Mr and Mrs Dhondy, making it a point whenever I was in Mombasa to have a meal with them. When in due course I married and brought the children down to Mombasa, our whole family would go and have lunch with them, their famous hospitality and generosity undiminished by the years. Rus, in the meantime, as we had expected, had joined the Army and was advancing in what all who knew him knew would be a distinguished career. Subsequently, he too married. I did not know his wife, as he had met her much after I had left Bombay.

Over the next many years, Mr and Mrs Dhondy would give me news of Rus's promotions, and their faces would glow as they shared his successes with me, someone close to them. But the success and elan with which Rus discharged his duties was not only a matter of family pride. It had become public knowledge by the time of the Bangladesh War. Rus was one of the heroes of the capture of Dhakka and a decorated officer, with such duties as reflected the exceptional confidence that the high command reposed in him. Far away in Nairobi, where we, with confused loyalties, held confused debates on the morning papers of those war months, it was not infrequently that I would intervene with my claim to know well a figure of that victory.

It was therefore with foreboding, having received the news from others, that I left for Mombasa to see Mr and Mrs Dhondy. When they opened the door, they stared at me as if I was their missing son. Then their wounded faces broke down.

'Where is he? Where is he?'

But I could not answer. I would not know. After the war, Rus had been posted back to head-quarters, and his family had joined him. They had resumed peacetime routine at the station. One morning at daybreak, as he always did, he went for his daily run. He did not come back. The regiment went to look for him. They could not find him. They found a few of his clothes later. But they did not find him. They did not find any remains or trace of him. Mr and Mrs Dhondy had flown out immediately to India. They made every effort, sought every assistance, but there was no resolution of the loss. Every institution that could, did carry out a most thorough investigation of the circumstances and spared no effort to find out what had happened. But their support too had been fruitless. After several months, Mr and Mrs Dhondy had returned home to Mombasa empty-hearted.

For many years after that, as my work took me to Mombasa I would always go to them for a meal. There on the table would be the same favourite dishes I had been given all those years ago. 'I know this is what you like,' Mrs Dhondy would invariably say. As I would enter their flat, Mr Dhondy would clutch at me as I embraced him, and as we would move towards the sofa and armchairs, the back of his hand would wipe a cheek, the handsome outline no longer sharp. We would then sit down, and the bottle of cold beer waiting for me would be opened ceremoniously. How are you, son, he would ask. Was the family alright? How was I doing? He was so happy he had seen my name and photograph in the news-papers last week, yes, he was so happy he had seen my name and photograph in the newspapers last week.

Then we would open the albums that had also been kept ready, and we would go through the photographs again. 'This was his first uniform.' 'This was outside your Bombay hostel.' 'This was when you two were in Panchgani,' pointing to the wrong photograph because of the blur in his eyes. 'This was…'

August 1947

HE PUT DOWN the file. The papers of tomorrow's court case were spread out on the small table on which they ate. It was a colonial prosecution in a colonial court and he was the advocate for the accused person. He rubbed his eyes and leaned back. The late night silence surfaced around him, and he allowed himself to relax for a few moments. He looked up and around, and his glance strayed to the newspapers on the stool next to him. The *East African Standard* of the past few days lay there in an untidy heap. He looked at the photograph on the page facing him, a scene of crowds and floodlit Saracen domes. He thought back to the past few days.

Government Road had been lit up. Not by the usually dim street lamps of Nairobi, but by the headlamps of the large number of motor cars that had moved bumper to bumper for hours from one end of the road to the other. His neighbour

Balraj Handa had a car, and both families had squeezed in and they had gone into town. All of them had thus become part of this queue of rejoicing. The shop windows were themselves celebratory lights. Whole streetfronts, on both sides, shone. Hundreds were strolling on the streets at this quite unusual hour, full of wonder at the displays in window after window. Many of these glowed orange, white and green, coloured crepe paper over weak electric lights, simulating the tricolour. Others displayed gaudy and improbable Taj Mahals as symbols of what was happening. Ornately framed photographs of the Mahatma and the new Prime Minister stood in the windows, smothered with garlands, a medley of leaves and flowers, fresh and wilted. The pavements with their protective overhang were full of decorations—bunting hung and paper triangles proliferated over the old wooden signs that said 'United Grocers - All Upper Class Delicacies', or 'Bharmal Tejpar & Co. - For Your Van Heusen Shirts'.

But that special night no one cared for the slogans of commerce or the incongruous sales talk of ill-dressed cloth merchants importuning buyers for the stylish products of foreign sweatshops. That night there was an urge to be together, to be where it was acknowledged by that togetherness that something special was happening, and that they were part of it. They were oblivious to the irony that this was a celebration of the demise of empire in a remnant heart of it, to which even now many sahibs were moving. That was an assertion of the latter's belief that though they may have had to leave India, they could find a home in Kenya, because there at least British colonial rule would remain for generations to come. And Settler Kenya obliged that belief, contrary and anachronistically to what was happening both within the country and in the fast-changing world around it. It was positioning the colony for a conflict that in five short years would erupt in tragedy.

They had walked up and down, and when at nine-thirty that memorable midnight hour *had* struck far away, car horns had blared and people had kept smiling. Finally near eleven, they had got back into the car and Balraj had taken them all back home to Desai Road, too excited to have felt that the evening was over.

The newspapers had followed. His eye returned to the *Standard*. Below the photograph the speech was reported. He had marked it out, and the words now rose to him. *'Long years ago we made a tryst with destiny, and now the time comes when we shall redeem our pledge…'* The words surged with the huge exultation of the hundreds of millions they had been spoken for. He turned his head away, holding back the involuntary tears. The words had redeemed with eloquent pride, confidence and hope the cost and carnage of the years of struggle. Insignificant, far away and unknown to the speaker, he yet felt a part of those words. *'At the stroke of the midnight hour, when the world sleeps…'* life and freedom had come. He thought, inconsequentially, that those latter had come to him too, here, even though he was yet one of a subject people in this shabby quarter of a still colonized town.

He looked down. *'A moment comes, which comes but rarely in history, when we step out from the old to the new, when an age ends, and when the soul of a nation, long suppressed, finds utterance.'* He shivered slightly, and then became conscious of the winter air. He wrapped the old shawl around him tighter, but could not look away. *'We have endured all the pains of labour and our hearts are heavy with the memory of this sorrow. Some of the pains continue even now.'*

The lorries had driven those nights round and round the civil service and railway housing estates close by his home, the vehicles packed with standing Sikhs and Punjabis chanting *'Hindustan Zindabad',* long live India. They had been carrying large flags, the saffron and green fluttering in the wind. He had wondered how these flags had reached Nairobi in time for the celebration. People had come out to gather in the night and cheer them. But those in the lorries had also been carrying hockey sticks, and *lathis,* and people had also heard other chants from them. As the trucks passed by, went round the estates, and kept returning and passing by again, those *other* chants had remained in the air, *'Pakistan Murdabad',* death to Pakistan. And other lorries had driven in and had chanted *'Pakistan Zindabad',* and they too had the other chant, *'Hindustan Murdabad'*. These were echoes of the distorted voices from the great events that were taking place so far away. Such cries had also crossed the black waters, he thought, and here too we had learnt, if not how to hate, at least how to pretend to hate, a step that often had the same consequences.

He shook his head and sighed. He turned to the file. It was a charge of sedition in the magistrate's court at Kiambu, *King versus Kimani s/o Theuri*. But even though he was just beginning in the legal profession, he could discern in the prosecution—in the use of the maximum sentence of seven years to put away local leaders, in the choice of apparently unknown accused persons to cut away at the grassroots of resistance, in the choice of a court outside Nairobi to stave off unwelcome publicity—systematic steps to deny his land its freedom.

The fountain pen bit into the writing pad as his defence submission for the morning took shape on the page.

Ndururu

RIVER ROAD in 1952 was a busy street. It had always been Nairobi's busiest street. Coolies, merchants of much ado and little profit, snake oil peddlers, layabouts, and hawkers of questionable commodities had long and in large numbers been its more prominent frequenters. High Government officials and community leaders were rare there.

It had therefore always seemed not just busy, but always filled with noise and ever uninvitingly crowded. Here people did not pass each other, they jostled their way through. This was not so on streets like Government Road or Delamere Avenue and the roads on that side of town. There people glided by, in muted converse. Physical contact was carefully avoided—by one lot from the fear or distaste of humiliating reprisals, by the other from the fear and distaste of contamination. For in this place, in this colony, if persons of every type were to be allowed on main streets or footpaths, they must yet not touch each other because colonialism separated people in space so that people separated themselves in their minds.

On River Road everything was untidy. Not that it was littered. That too. But that the shop fronts were dusty, the shop signs faded, the shop owners unwashed. The same number of people on Government Road looked purposeful, here they looked unruly. On River Road, there were few ties to be seen, shirt fronts hung out, unironed clothes covered passers-by, women shuffled, and the customers were seedy. River Road was not the address of emporia and delectable provision stores, only of ration shops and of tailors with their sewing machines, their sole possession, who sat in the shops of others.

When the street was first laid out, Nairobi's only hub was the railway station. Thus River Road's main entry point for many years was not from the Khoja Mosque end. It was from the Railway Station side. Its first dwellers and users therefore were coolies, 'time-expired coolies' (the malevolent label by which the Railway

Administration referred to ex-coolies who were staying on), carters, masons, itinerant salesmen and off-duty railway workers. They were loud in their exchanges with each other, and equally loud in their derision of ways different from those they had come from. But all that was a long time ago. Now in 1952, in the December of that year, though the street had not been cleaned up and an unkempt thoroughfare still met all who ventured in, yet a subtle change had taken place.

*

In a *duka* on that street, a man sat cross-legged on a low dais on the floor of his shop, his wares all around him. In one piece, the dais was a seat for him, a watchtower against shoplifters, and a counter over which to receive payment and pass goods. His name was Ndururu. His overenthusiastic concern for every cent, the smallest coinage then in general use, had given him his name. If he had any other, it was certain that no one remembered it, and very likely that he too had lost any recollection of it.

A customer halted and pointed. Ndururu leaned over, and with a metal scoop expertly retrieved almost exactly the quantity demanded. He lifted a small square of yellowed newspaper to deputize for wrapping. His hands barely moved and, as if by itself, the paper swivelled into a cone container. In a single movement Ndururu poured the measured item into it, tapped the packet smartly, licked a brown gum strip to seal the packet top, and stretched out to the customer in silent exchange, the packet in the customer's hand, for a coin in Ndururu's palm. He looked at it, even though the weight had told him, unseen, that the correct sum had been paid. He tossed the coin accurately into the open till beside him.

Hour after hour in the hot morning, Ndururu repeated this ritual. Sometimes he tossed the coins into the till, sometimes it appeared that he missed the drawer of the till and the coins landed on a cloth beside it. Sometimes after a transaction, he reached out and turned over the cloth, sometimes he left it as it was. Some customers bought soap, some maize flour, others sugar or lentils. Some bought spices, for in the streets running down to the river were those like him, who cooked with these spices. Some bought a sweet.

A man on the opposite pavement watched. He was leaning against a dark doorway, anonymous in his immobility. Midway in this pattern, Ndururu got up, stretched and turned to the back wall of the shop. He pushed against a sheet of dun cloth on which a display of *khangas* had been pinned. The sheet gave way, revealing the outline of a shut door. Ndururu went through to the dark interior. The man on the other side of the road moved. He crossed the street smoothly, and sidled through the passing pedestrians to the shop.

He strained forward over the low counter and looked carefully all over the shop, peering into the corners. He stared at the open drawer of the till. Copper coins looked back, an odd bit of faded silver among them. There were no notes. The cloth next to it was innocent of any coins. Ndururu re-entered quietly, carrying a hurricane lantern and a jar of sweets. The man gave a start, and took a step back as if to walk away. Then he stood his ground, and taking out a fifty-cent piece, asked for twine. Ndururu stood up again and, retrieving a ball of it, expertly spun the string around his palm a few times and cut it. He handed it over and, as he resumed his seat, tossed the coin into the open drawer.

The man turned away and merged into the swirl of moving pedestrians. But after a while he was back on the other side, unobtrusive again, this time along the side of a sweetmeats shop. For another two hours he watched Ndururu's shop. Housewives came and took packets away, men came with empty sodawater bottles. Ndururu would use a tin funnel and pour in kerosene. A customer came and bought the hurricane lantern. Persons kept buying sweets.

At some time in the afternoon, the watcher on the other side of the street left. River Road had slowed a little in the heat, but continued its business. After sunset, Ndururu stopped for the day and closed the big doors facing the road. By a faint bulb, he emptied the drawer and counted his takings. Then he lifted the cloth beside the till and picked up all the coins he had pushed under it from time to time. He counted these, the takings of the sweets and some other items he had sold that day, and made a separate tally.

He wrapped small heaps of these coins in paper and again in bits of cloth, making them into small soundless bundles. He picked up one of his small paper bags, ones made by him gluing together magazine pages. He poured in a bit of maize flour, then stuffed in the packages of coins. He poured in more flour, folded the top and tied up the bag securely with string. Tomorrow, the messenger would come and 'buy' the flour, so collecting the contributions he had received today. Today, the messenger had taken them in the lantern. He picked up the packet, stood up and sighed. He went into the back of the house.

*

At the same moment, at Kingsway Police Station, Inspector Hardy was labouring over the correct words for his report to the OCS, the Officer Commanding the Station. So far he had written: '*On my instructions our informer has proceeded to the shop called 'River Road Provision Stores' (Sole propr. Chandulal Amarchand Patel), for the past two weeks and has been watching the same. He has been giving a daily report. From these reports no evidence of any collection of money for the Mau Mau appears to be taking place. The informer's evidence points to commercial transactions common to this class of shop, with no unusual customers apparent. No suspicious connections have been traced. I have accordingly paid off No.NBO/CONF/12, and unless you consider that surveillance should be continued, I request your concurrence that I instruct him not to resume.'*

He read it again. Feeling he could not improve upon it any more, he signed it, put the date and tagged the report. With the file under his arm, he walked into the corridor to the Chief Inspector's office.

Emergency

2002

'*CŪCŪ* WANJA, you wear this old *leso* all the time. It's all torn now. You can't even see the face on it any more. Who is it? Throw it away,' the young women affectionately teased the old lady who sat quietly among them at the stadium, for the town homecoming of the new President.

*

1965

'Excellency, they are pressing. You have not been to their side since *Uhuru*. They want to see you. So they have come all this way. You did not see them in Nairobi when they came last year.'

He waved the argument away.

'You had told them that you would see them the next time they came.' He turned, annoyed at the persistence. 'I don't want to see them.' He knew what they wanted to say, to *demand*.

'Their leaders have petitions. They have brought a choir and dancers for you. They could become a problem, Excellency, you should see them.'

His face showed his exasperation. Then it cleared. 'Ask them to perform tonight. As for the petitions, *you* collect them and deal with them.'

*

He came into the open arena in good humour. Mombasa in these August evenings was very pleasant. The food had been good and the sycophancy at table adequate.

At first he listened to the songs and the music and noted the due praise to him that the words contained. He smiled in approval. He continued listening briefly and laughed and clapped at the barbs that the songs threw at the white colonialists now gone. Then he lost interest. In a while, other songs began, carrying the messages he was refusing to receive in personal audience. They spoke of *uhuru*, what people had fought for, and how so many had died; how others had come back to find lands lost and wives taken. And could something be done about all this by the one who was the Father of the Nation, the saviour of the country, the one whom all loved and admired unceasingly. He had not been listening.

From the makeshift dais he watched, in desultory fashion, the groups on the cleared ground before him. One of them, dancing and singing for him now, moved forward and backward, the steps bringing them closer to him, then away. Suddenly, he became conscious of one of the dancers looking at him markedly. The man was tall, thin, angular, with no talent for dance, but still being deferred to by the rest of that small group even as they moved around him in more graceful fashion.

From the past, seeping back came recall of the man. But that was epochs away, when there had been no independence, no prime ministership, no presidency. Not just epochs away, lives away, we were different people. 'No,' the man's eyes said, 'we were the same people. *We* are the same people.' And the man's eyes also asked, 'Who are *you* now?' And the rhythmic stamp of their feet was repeating, 'The Emergency is not over; the Emergency is not over.'

Those were not lives of epochs away. This was now August 1965, and those times were only thirteen years away, only thirteen out of his seventy-four, a manageable piece, only the recent past, easy to summon up. Only thirteen years ago at Thomson's Falls. In a bar, with others, giving him information, arranging the next public meeting, the next set of people to hear and instruct in back rooms, the beer served by Rebecca, it all came flooding back.

And the years before that, all the time, everywhere, Kandara, Ndumberi, Ol Kalou, Molo, Pumwani, wherever the police were not; moving him, shielding him, arguing with him, urging him. But he had not listened to the man.

He had found suddenly that the man had become necessary to his own movement. Where was he from? Was he from some central committee he did not know of? He never learnt.

Then the man had disappeared. Into the

forest? Into the city? Into a police station? Into screening for oathing? Into a detention camp? Into a rehabilitation pipeline? He did not know. And had not thought to ask.

He dammed it all back. For him there was no time before this. This now, was the only time. And this was the only him. Not the failing half-drunkard of the pre-Emergency years, not the absentee self-exile in Britain; he could have come back then, no one had stopped him, no arrest had awaited him. But in England one could talk anti-colonialism, or if some wanted it, anti-imperialism. And go on paid trips to different countries.

Now, he thought, there was only the all-consuming present, of which he could not get enough. This was *uhuru*. There was no time for the past. It took away from the worthwhile things he was doing now: taking back the land from those once-arrogant settlers, squeezing money from those cheating shopkeepers, giving favours to our people. Were all these not the programme we had agreed on years ago, the programme of freedom? Had I also not gone to prison? Was I not keeping the pact made only two years ago with the British? They look after me; I look after them. After all, they protect their strategic interests, I protect ours. Who are these people in rags to question me? What do they know of high negotiations and private arrangements, about things bigger than our small country?

Who were they to say I was the breaker of the pact that I had made with my people? I kept it, I brought them Independence. That was what they wanted, wasn't it? What more did they want? Now it was up to them.

The President dropped his eyes and turned away. His revulsion at the unspoken demand of those eyes became physical. He shrugged his shoulders though he was speaking to no one. I have done enough for them. What did they do for me? During the years at Lokitaung and Lodwar? During the years I was wasting uselessly for them? He made a face to himself. It answered him, 'Nothing.'

The tall man moved back in ungainly steps, silently within the shrill voices of the men and women singing and turning around him, and merged into them. The President looked away abruptly. After a while the dance stopped. One woman bobbed. The men stood uncertainly. Some made an awkward bow. Then all walked off in clumsy fashion into the darkness. The tall man last.

The President leaned back to the Comptroller, smiling through the resurge of his anger. 'See that this lot gets some extra beer. Give them...more meat, beds...,' he hesitated, then his eye caught the *lesos* draped on the tables beside him. They carried his portrait. He extended his hand and pulled two of them up. 'Here, give them *these*.' Then, 'Also something. Not too much.' And as his ill-humour continued, he called out after the Comptroller. 'But no land!' He began snickering loudly at what he considered fine malice for the court to enjoy. Those nearby did, in subservient echo.

As the next group performed, he got up suddenly and left.

One of the Comptroller's junior staff came to the back to give the group money, extra beer and the *lesos*, and to show them where the food was and where they could sleep. Having done what he had been given orders to do and could say he had done, he left them to themselves. The tall man looked at the money. It did not fill his large bony palm. Neither the pain of the past ten years nor anger flickered anywhere on his face. Impassively, he passed it on to Wanja, the treasurer of their troupe. She had been with him in the forests. She took it as silently. She passed one of the *lesos* to the other woman dancer, and kept one for herself.

East Africans

IT WAS past midnight, the talk carrying on unabated. It was the middle of what they called Spring Semester, but what we knew was really the middle of winter. We were East Africans abroad, all on scholarships at different law schools, coming together at Harvard Law in early 1975 for a seminar on law and development in Africa.

The outside was a distasteful cold. The Yard was heavily embroidered at its edges with trampled snow. Those emptying on the late hour from booked periods on the old computer frames of those days, and from the several libraries around, did not stop to converse in the freezing air. It was the end of the meeting's first day. The sessions had lingered on more than we thought seemly, for we were of the unspoken but unanimous opinion that such events were only to be pleasant reunions, a break from the heavy work at the schools, not an extension of it.

We had finished dinner and had retired to the Common Room put at our disposal. A warm camaraderie sheltered us from the weather. A generous availability of beer and the distance from home united us. The last session had generated some debates, and the arguments were now spilling over.

'The book is good, no matter what you fellows said in the afternoon.'

'No, a book on law and constitution in Uganda cannot be published at this time. There is no law and no working constitution in Uganda now,' Mahesh Patel replied.

Otieno Okoyo's deep voice intervened. 'There is no time when a book on law and constitution is not of value, and ergo, no time when it cannot be published.'

'But what purpose would it serve beyond recording the author's efforts? Very commendable, no doubt.'

'There will come a time when we will have ended this infamous episode in our history, and then more than ever will we be in need of a book like this,' said Bii.

'I think to publish it now is to validate Idi Amin as representing Ugandan law and constitutionalism. This is not the time for books for the future. This is the time for steps to ensure that Amin goes. Amin should go,' cried Mahesh.

'I don't think it is Idi Amin who is bad. It is the people around him,' responded Bii.

'No, no, no,' Sserumaga intervened emphatically, banging down his glass. 'Let me tell you. There should be no mistake. The problem is not around him. The problem is him.'

'No state is one man,' the deep voice returned from the armchair. 'Least of all, Idi Amin.' A pause. 'Or Louis XIV. Clarify your thinking. Go through Engels' correspondence on this. You should read my book *The Nature of the State in Uganda*. It is forthcoming.'

'We should have read the signs when that Commission on the gold from the Congo was on.'

'Well, Obote too was involved in that business. We should not think that Obote was any better. That was good riddance I'd say.'

'Well, it may not be a popular view now,' said

Bii, 'but if I had to choose, I should prefer him over the lawless individuals we have now.'

Kwame, present by reason of his ongoing research on beer rather than any special interest in East African law or development, interrupted his drink enough to say, 'You lot have paid no attention to the damage we have done ourselves in West Africa, and have learnt nothing from us. You'd better take a closer look before you go our serial way from election to coup and back. And forth!'

'True,' Otieno Okoyo grunted, 'the Continent has seen struggles. But not always to freedom. In some places, we have moved only to tyranny.'

'This is not what the struggle for *uhuru* was about. What you do not understand,' said Mahesh, answering Bii, 'is that the dominant forces here are not Idi Amin. Amin is not an aberration. He is the result of structures that were put in place by neo-colonial forces. Idi Amin is a disaster for Uganda, the region and the continent. He must be removed.'

'Exactly. He must go,' said Sserumaga. 'I agree with Mahesh.'

In the lull, Okoyo said dreamily, 'The good thing about tyranny is that it is transient.'

Sserumaga ignored him. 'Amin has betrayed Uganda. He has betrayed the people of Uganda. He betrayed me.'

We all knew that last year Idi Amin had dismissed Sserumaga from his high office of Deputy Attorney-General (Parliamentary) and had thrown him out of Uganda. Sserumaga had reached Nairobi with nothing to his name and even less in prospects. He had wandered around looking for work. He could not appear in court. He could not get other jobs. His income became anti-Amin seminars. He went, on handouts, to Dar es Salaam to find some unofficial form of asylum there. He spoke when he could on the oppression and criminality of the Amin regime at university gatherings and to the diplomatic corps. He appeared in the newspapers. He became well known as an exile opposing Amin, and as one standing up for human rights and freedoms in Uganda. Eventually, supportive people in East Africa and New York, seeking ways to assist anti-Amin forces, offered him a scholarship to do his master's in the US, on the oppression and criminal nature of the Amin regime. His maintenance and transport would also be paid.

'We know that, old chap,' said Bii sympathetically. 'This is a bad time for Uganda.'

'See what he has done to me after all that I did for him. After all, I was the one who drafted the Asian expulsion laws he wanted when no one else would. He must go. I agree with Mahesh,' Sserumaga repeated, putting an arm around Mahesh Patel's shoulder in anti–Idi Amin solidarity.

The Minister's Visit

THE MINISTER BURST into the small room. Lackeys, sycophants and the department officials tumbled in behind him. The three officials seated in the office looked up apprehensively.

'Who are you?' said the Minister with bluff bonhomie to the one nearest him.

The man jumped up. 'I am Onguto. Sir.'

'No, no,' laughed the Minister. 'I mean what do you do here?'

'I am the Water Accountant, sir.'

'Good, good. And you?' he said to the one sitting on the other side of the table.

'I-I-I am his ass-s-sistant, s-sir.'

'I hope you are checking everything.'

The man kept nodding.

The Minister turned to the other desk. The man there said, 'I send out the bills, sir.'

The Minister looked at desk opposite. There was no one seated at it. But draped on the back

of the empty chair hung a jacket. Everyone followed his gaze. There was complete silence. The
Minister turned to the Council Director. The
Minister nodded towards the coat. 'You see, you
see.'

'Yes, yes,' said the Director.

The Minister turned. The crowd behind
leaned forward expectantly. The Minister looked
back at the empty chair. There was a hush. Then
he announced.

'He's fired.'

There was a buzz of satisfaction. One of the
more ingratiating followers attempted a clap. The
Minister had performed again. He was not called
the New Broom for nothing. He embodied the
determination of this new government to be different from the past twenty-four years. He moved
to the door, the small crowd around him falling
over to get out of his way.

In the corridor, the Minister moved at his
brisk pace. Over his shoulder he threw instructions at the Director, who was scurrying to keep
up. 'That will show all of them we mean business.
When we say…'

The Director ran a little faster to keep within earshot.

'...that we are serious about serving the people. We don't want any more corruption.'

'Yes, yes,' said the Director as they proceeded with the rest of the inspection.

Later, in the afternoon, the Director returned to the Water office. 'Who sits there?' he demanded, pointing to the offending chair, which stared back, still unoccupied.

'Mr Wanyanga, sir. The Accounts Inspector. But he's on leave. He went on leave last week.'

'Then whose jacket was that on his chair?' cried the Director.

'It was a visitor's, sir. He was seeing Mr Mwatete here.'

'But then where was the visitor?'

'He had gone to the toilet, sir.'

The Director drew a long breath. Then left. It was, he rehearsed his letter of explanation in his mind, a 'misunderstanding', one of those things. Anyway, that was that.

But it turned out it was not.

At the Heads of Department meeting the

next morning, the Minister appeared. During the tea break he spoke to the Director. 'Well, Mr Director. We meet again. How are you today?'

'Alright, sir, alright.'

'So how's our little matter of yesterday?' The Minister *had* remembered.

'Alright, sir, alright, sir.'

'Have you served that man with his letter of dismissal?'

The Director hesitated.

The Minister continued, 'We need to make an example of such fellows. They come in, leave their jackets about, and then rush out to look after their own businesses. They think we don't know? Those days are over.'

'Yes, yes, of course, sir.'

'We are not like that past government…'

'No, no,' muttered the Director, who had enthusiastically served that very past government for twenty years, and had benefited greatly by the services he had rendered to certain prominent individuals in it.

'We must clean up, and clean up soon. Isn't that so?'

'Yes, yes.'

'So send off that letter soon.'

'Yes, sir.'

'Well, do it, do it.'

'Of course, sir.'

The Minister thought for a moment. 'Actually, send me a copy tomorrow morning. I have another inspection out of town in the afternoon. I'll use it there.' The Minister laid down his cup. 'You've been doing well at the city council. Keep it up. We might need you higher up.' He patted the Director on the arm in friendly fashion and moved on.

The rest of the morning passed for the Director in rushes of panic. There was no fault, there could be no dismissal. Could he send such a letter then? Might he be needed higher up? Conflicting emotions swirled in his mind. But as the meeting broke up at lunch, he was resolved.

When he reached the Council, he called his secretary in. 'Bring me Mr Wanyanga's file.' He dictated, 'The Council regrets to inform you that your services are herewith summarily terminated due to dereliction of duty.' As she rose, he gave further instructions, 'Make the usual copies for Personnel and make a special copy for the Minister himself.'

Signing the letter, he kept the copy to the Minister. Tomorrow morning, he would himself give it to him. The Minister would then know that he was an officer who could be relied on. The Minister would keep him in mind for the future, for higher things. Many positions were opening up in the new administration, and they would increasingly have need of reliable and trustworthy officers, experienced officers ready to carry out orders efficiently without too many questions. Handing over the letter himself would be a quick assurance to the Minister of these qualities, and, he thought, he must continue to find ways for the Minister to be reminded that he was available.

Two weeks later, Mr Wanyanga returned from his leave and found the letter on his desk.

First Pay Cash

THE SHADOWS FRACTURED the patch of sunlight that reached into the dim shop. Vinod noted the intrusions without any enthusiasm and did not stir. The shop itself was a family leftover in a quiet edge of Nairobi. It was a low wood and corrugated iron structure of the early colonial days, built long before the present uninterested occupants were born. It was on the wrong side of a corner of the main road, and the old building had improbably survived close to a century into 1993.

The *duka*, its promiscuous display of wares, even the windowless gloom habitually surrounding the long wooden counter worn uneven by many decades of use and neglect, has now become a national institution. In the past it had been the symbol of other concerns—of prejudice and a contrary envy on one part, and of an unattractive racial scorn and grasping, on the other.

But now being a *dukawalla*, the same vilified occupation, has become a principal ambition of the same many whose resentments had in the past protested its existence. The old template is being applied in all the exploding urban sprawls that have blighted the country in the years since independence, multiplying the *duka*'s availability manifold. The old ones remain, often with the very same counters in the very same buildings, only now disfigured by meshes of metal all over the premises, feeble protection against armed robbery, reflections of the collapse of public trust in our country.

One of the shadows spoke. 'Do you sell machetes?' Vinod stared indifferently at the men. They did not look like his usual customers. He said nothing.

'Do you sell machetes?'

At last Vinod responded. 'What is that?'

'Machetes,' the man repeated. His hands moved to assist the explanation. 'To cut trees. Crops.'

Vinod thought for a while. He did not have whatever-it-was that the man had asked for. But he would not allow a customer to go away untempted by something else. He sighed, got up from the worn wooden armchair his father had left him after a lifetime's rough use, and went into the back room. Returning, he said, 'We only have this,' and dropped the item on the counter between them.

'That *is* a machete,' said the man.

'That is a *panga*,' said Vinod.

'How much is it?'

Vinod, who could recite the price of every single item on the shelves, counters, overladen walls, floor and ceiling of the shop, made a show of studying the bit of paper stuck on the long blade. He repeated the figure off-handedly.

'Do you have one hundred of these?'

Within Vinod's habitual and deep inertia, a brief surprise stirred. This unfamiliar feeling and an inarticulateness born of an imperfect education combined into an untypical response, 'Why you want hundred?'

The man turned to his companion, who had been silent so far. They looked at each other for a moment. Then the companion turned to Vinod and spoke for the first time.

'We have a lot of cutting to do.' He smiled.

Vinod knew he did not have such a quantity, but he would bring out whatever he did have.

At that moment the shop assistant passed between Vinod and the men, carrying tinned goods for the shelves. Some slipped, clattering on the floor. Vinod was caught between his reflex to serially and publicly reprimand every lapse in his employees, and his recognition that interruption could compromise what sounded like a profitable transaction here. Habit prevailed. His voice rose, 'How many times have I told you not to do it this way?' Then turning back to the men, he said softly, 'I will see how many I have.'

He returned to the counter with an armful.

'Just now I have these. When you want hundred? I can get them.'

The men consulted. The quiet one said, 'We will come next week.'

By the time they came the following week, Vinod was ready with the delivery. As they left with their purchase, they confirmed a further similar order.

They came in this way for a few weeks, content with Vinod's service. Towards the end of the year, as they were taking their usual delivery, they said, 'We want another thousand.'

Vinod's mind raced to calculate the profit he would be entitled to. Then slowed, to work out the logistics of such a number. He would have to see the main agent in the city and find out how this could be done. The agent would ask for payment. Vinod blurted out, 'But you have to pay cash first.'

The man acknowledged the demand with a brief shake of the head, murmuring to himself. Then, more loudly to Vinod, he said, 'We will not be coming; can you send them to us?'

Vinod, who never made deliveries, nodded vigorously. 'Where shall I send them?'

The man handed him a slip of paper. 'It is written there. To Kigali.'

Dukawalla

IT WAS the turn of the century. There was an air of change about. Anything seemed possible. And when he had taken the decision to leave home and travel far, he had felt sure that he was going to prosper. And here he was, set up as a trader in a new place.

Quiet and sparsely peopled, it was quite different from the crowded towns at home. The landscape was unfamiliar. He had had to take a train, his first, to the nearest station on the line, and then had travelled another day to this small place. There had been troubles both in this region and around, with several killings. This was rough territory, but it had settled down, and he often asked himself, where were there no troubles? Remaining at home in a large family, he would have looked forward only to further poverty. Moving out, he had grasped at the chance of a better future.

He had opened a small *duka* and filled it with the merchandise of daily living, and quiet hope. All his time was spent in it, patiently serving whatever custom came in. It was in a low corrugated iron building belonging to another person from his home town, a pioneer here. This was the person who had brought him over and had encouraged him to start here. He had listened to this man who, on a visit home, spoke of the opportunities here, and who had asked his father to send him up. When he did finally come, the man rented him the single shop area, gave him some goods on credit, and forced him to buy all the rest. His mentor drove a hard bargain, even with his own protégé.

The settlement was small. Close by was the DC's *boma*. This was the most important place in the town. The District Commissioner sometimes came into his shop and bought items that had to be sent up to his residence. Outside, in the unpaved street, a shallow gutter of earth ran past his shop and the other buildings, petering out in the mud behind.

Earning was a slow, cumulative process, but

he was ready to persevere. Others before him, he
knew, had, within twenty years or even less, become rich and built a stone house for themselves.
He was content to follow their path. To bring
in as much as he could, he kept the *duka* open
late till nine each night. He would then carefully
close the wide doors of the shop and lock up from
outside, and coming back through the back door,
the inside as well. He would fall asleep under the
counter on a mixture of blankets and cardboard.
Hot though the place was during the day, it
turned cold in the nights.

Here he was a stranger. His small community
consisted of his family and that of his mentor. By
journeys in different directions, they could meet
other traders who were also from where they
came, or at least spoke the same language even if
from other villages. A few times a year they would
meet and spend a day together. The cooking
would be in larger quantities of their own food,
and the women would not stop talking in their
own language, not needing to hesitantly form local words or decipher the local responses. Scarce
as these reunions were, and he thought of them as

reunions, they yet drew comments from his hosts about how he and his people always kept together and would not mix with the locals.

In the early years in the long intervals between these get-togethers, he was often alone in his house. From time to time his wife returned to her parents' home. Then there was no one to whom he could speak in his own language, and sometimes he found that he was talking to himself.

He had spent enough time here, though, to have picked up the local language. He spoke it in broken fashion. This was noted by the people around. They would sometimes correct him. But the flow of their language was alien to him, and despite his best efforts he was not able to shake off his fractured grammar and his strong accent. Often after an altercation with them, on prices or change for instance, he would hear his customers imitating him maliciously as they moved away dissatisfied.

Here in the distant countryside far from the capital, there was not much to do. He often felt lonely. The road was seldom in good condition. When the rains came they further isolated an already far-off place, and he felt even more cut off than usual. He had settled here, and the years had passed. But he still had reservations. He found reasons to send the family off to relatives at home. Or was this now home? He kept changing his conclusions on this. When their eldest, a boy, had reached school-going age, he and his wife had felt that the only school here was not good enough. The child had been sent back. When their second, a girl, had reached the same age, they had felt that this remote place was unsafe for a young girl. They had sent her away too. The others had followed, for similar, or similarly contrived, reasons.

And it seemed that of late members of the family had left more often and for longer periods. There seemed an atmosphere now that had not been there before. When he had first come, the local people had viewed him as a stranger, but not as an intruder. When, after his first year, he had gone back home and returned with his new bride, he had often been asked, 'Why don't you marry from here? Why do you bring in a wife from foreign places?' As his mentor too had earlier done exactly what he had, he was often

told, 'You people always keep yourselves aloof
and apart from us.' He could neither explain it
nor find anything wrong in what he had done. So
he kept silent whenever the subject came up. By
not answering them, he made them feel justified.
He thus found himself confirming the odd fact
that injustice makes one inarticulate rather than
the opposite. But in these past few months, he
had found that the same remarks had sounded
less like comments and more like accusations.

In the mornings the intermittent business often found him leaning against the counter chas-
ing away the small boys who would jump into
the shop from the mud-floored verandah, trying
in small groups to distract him and pick up whatever sweets they could. Outside the shop, several
of the town's old men would be on a bench, some
regulars, others invited for the day. But these days
he had also seen much younger men coming up
to, and spending time with, the old men.

In the late evening after he closed the shop, he
usually kept to himself. The language of the social
groups was difficult for him, but he also felt that
he had nothing in common with them. When his

wife was here, she found the same impediments, and the two of them tended to spend their time in the house. His wife felt uneasy during the day and insecure in the dark. Attacks at night had been common, but these had always been between the locals themselves, or between the locals and neighbouring tribes. He and his wife had always said to themselves, 'These people are like that.' But now the threat seemed directed at them.

In the earlier days, he remembered, there had been policemen sent up from the provincial headquarters. The DC then had been interested in establishing the authority of the centre. But now the town's remoteness had re-established itself.

The situation had changed. As time had passed, agitators, calling themselves politicians, were emerging in the town. They asked for self-rule for themselves. He never understood this. On the rare occasions on which he thought about it, he always wondered whether they were ready for this self-government that they talked about. They congregated in the bar opposite the *duka* and simply talked for hours on end. 'They are only drunkards,' was his secret thought. But he noticed that they were becoming bolder in their rhetoric and in their conduct. Originally they would come to the shop respectfully and would pay for the small purchases they made. But now, for the past year, they had been making speeches that had disturbed him.

One time at a small meeting on the town's brown dust bowl that was its football field, one of the locals had come from out of town. He had spoken against exploiters who were looting the town's people and the economy. The speaker had said that such people had come to take away the land and deny the locals business, and should be thrown out immediately. He had said that it was time that these businesses were in the hands of the local people. This was their birthright and could not be taken away. He had made other similar remarks.

The speaker had gone away the same day, but those words had generated months of talk against him and his mentor all around the small town. One day during this period, there had been a dispute with some customers about the amount of flour he had packed in the paper bag. The argument had become heated and soon attracted a large audience. Together with the accusations of short-changing his customers, he was told, 'You are a foreigner and should get out of here.'

He had ignored all this at first. In any case, he could not speak up. No one listened to him here, and he felt that no one believed he had any answer. He felt as if he had been the subject of long discussions by them over a long time, all in his absence, and that an unalterable conclusion of condemnation had already been reached. He felt any remonstrance was useless. Sometimes he had felt he should protest to the Government about this treatment, but his English was not very good either, and he had dropped the idea. And now the young men would sometimes burst into his shop raucously, spend no money, and then when he cautiously asked them if they wanted to buy anything, would simply leave.

This had gone on for nearly a year, and he was a worried man. He had sent his wife back, and told whoever asked that one of the children was ill and had had to be looked after. In the past few weeks matters had got worse. One weekend, groups had gathered in town. After some time they had come over and, finding his shop open, begun demanding loudly that he close his shop. He was surrounded and unable to refuse. The next day the groups kept meeting and went to the DC and made demands. They demanded that all aliens must quit the town. They said that the land and the town belonged to the people who had always been there from olden times.

Then they came privately to his mentor. In the big shop, in a long meeting that he had attended, they told his mentor that all foreigners must leave within sixty days. They complained that when his people had come to the town, the Government had never compensated its residents, and that the Government was responsible for these aliens who had now occupied their land and that they were justified in evicting all such people.

He had been spending anxious nights after that. The whole of the following week, he had rushed to his mentor's shop at every opportunity—during the day when business was slack, and at night as soon as he had closed his shop. Over the flickering kerosene lamp, his mentor had reassured him.

'All this is just talk. I know senior persons among our people. I will speak to them. They will speak to the Government. They will quickly put a stop to this nonsense. The Government won't allow this. The Government has brought law and order here. We are protected. Without us these people would be nothing.'

In the past fortnight, as the sixty days drew to a close, his uneasiness had increased. As he moved occasionally in the town, he would hear remarks. 'Go back to your ancestral land, wherever it is.' Or, as if speaking to each other, 'We can smell them across a street.' The little boys would call out after him, '*Mwizi*, thief.'

When his mentor told him that he was leaving, he became even more concerned. But his mentor had again reassured him. 'I am going to Nairobi so I can make sure that policemen are sent out. All this will be stopped.' He did not believe that, and, uncharacteristically, had blurted out, 'But the Government never does anything for us. The Government does not like us. It never helps us.'

His mentor had merely smiled. 'We know people, big people,' the mentor said, patting him on his arm. 'You will see. I will return with a guard before their useless sixty days end.' Seeing that he remained unconvinced, his mentor had continued, 'Don't worry. Nothing will happen. You know these people. They just talk. They don't know anything else. Not like us.'

He was not comforted. It was a reluctant farewell that he bid when he saw his mentor go, carrying packed goods, which he was informed were being taken to be sold.

When the week was over, he waited anxiously for the return of his mentor. But there was no appearance from the latter. In the days that followed, his anxiety grew, as his mentor had still not returned. However, as the sixtieth day passed, and there were no confrontations, his anxiety abated a little. Looking for hostility he found none. Listening for a repetition of the remarks he had been subjected to over the past months, he found only civility. One evening he was even invited to the bar opposite the *duka*, where he found everybody drinking with the politician who was visiting the town again after many months. He felt uncomfortable about the drink. He himself did not drink. Neither his father nor his mother had ever had alcohol in their house. But with the invitation and the good humour around him, he felt for the first time in a while a relaxation of the tension that he had carried inside him so long. He smiled a lot, and held a glass of beer awkwardly for much of the evening, while all the locals talked to him and all the visitors ignored him.

The following night as he smelt the smoke, he had no premonition. But as he ran out, he heard, amidst the noise, the loud cries more distinctly, 'Foreigner', 'Return home', 'Get out'. As the pangas struck at him, Waithaka, thinking of his faraway family, fell.

A small item in the middle pages of the national newspapers of 7 July 2001 reported, '*A shopkeeper in West Pokot, Mr Waithaka Kimani, died yesterday in an arson attack on his shop. The victim was attacked by a gang that was armed with pangas. Nothing was taken and the gang fled. The Police have stated that they have opened investigations. The District Commissioner denied that any ethnic clashes had taken place, and stated that this was just a normal murder.'*

Makindu

AS ONE DRIVES into Makindu, the rural landscape appears Indian: barren, save for the waves of heat and the slow-moving bony cattle of dark herder men with thin legs. The only trees in the landscape are bleached shrubs. The only colour is glare. The skin keeps grazing itself against the sun. The endemic poverty leans against the mind. Whatever man does, however nature moves, dust rises. The memory of India and of the summer Punjab is obvious. When the road curves to unveil over the brow of the next hill a gleaming white temple, the resemblance is positively disconcerting.

Makindu came together as a settlement when the railway from Mombasa to Lake Victoria was being built at the turn of the century, and construction halted there to draw breath. At each hundred miles, the builders laid out a major station. The first was at Voi, a hundred miles from the starting point at Kilindini, Mombasa. Makindu was that at the end of the second hundred miles. In the first decade of that new century, Makindu was not the quiet siding that the passenger train now passes through in the night. It was then a bustling halt—a marshalling yard, a point of disembarkation for dinner, a police post, an estate of railway quarters. Train crews changed here. My grandfather's did. Engines took water. Passengers meals. What would become the Sikh Temple was then only a meeting room, a rough construct of corrugated iron and wooden beams, its present quality of tranquillity and benison unrevealed yet. There are still traces of all this from that past, including some scattered graves through which a road presently passes. The railway quarters which housed the changing staff stationed there are redundant now, mostly empty, old architectural relatives who are still in the homestead, but nobody really knows how they are related, or, any longer, even who they are.

The road from Nairobi to Mombasa in the 1950s was still murram, and the battered pickup laboured along it, dust flaring up behind. Borrowed from a not quite successful contractor, the vehicle shook on doggedly over the corrugated surface, the movement one continuous rattle. This did not bother the four occupants on its metal floor at the back. Charn Singh and Harnam were employees of the contractor, lent, like the pickup, for the trip. Kulwant Singh, though he himself was modestly unaware of it, was a master carpenter, whose bare planks of wood were pieces of fine art, his finished pieces much more. The fourth was a tall lanky boy, Sabjit, with a turban narrow like his young face, the latter adorned by a thin sparse beard. He was brought along to learn how to help whoever needed help, and in the process find his life-work, whether as electrician, woodworker, wheelwright or contractor, as yet a card not turned face upwards. They were the volunteers escorting the passenger in the seat in the cab. This was the priest from Nairobi.

They had woken up early and had been travelling for hours now in that slow vehicle on that bad road. Their turbans were dusty in every crease, their beards red with the earth blowing around them, their frayed clothes stained further. Occasionally, they overtook an even slower car, a few with only the front seats occupied. Then the four would keep looking at them, fascinated by the extraordinary sight of only two persons in a whole car. In the parts of Nairobi the four frequented, no car ever carried fewer than seven persons, and usually all the laps were filled too. That the passengers they were passing looked well groomed and clean on this road was glamour, and the four would stare back at the receding car. Sometimes from within, the occupants would then wave extravagantly at them. Before they would become conscious of the malice, the four would find themselves waving back foolishly, at strangers they did not know, of a shade they knew did not want to know them.

They stopped briefly at Sultan Hamud, where once the then Sultan of Zanzibar had visited railhead. The station had thus been named after him. Their own pickup's visit with less exalted personages would not be so commemorated, and it simply filled up petrol. The attendant pumped the handle back and forth as the meter turned to record the gallon they had asked for. They screwed back the petrol tank cap and continued.

After Simba, the first drift appeared, and they slowed down. The road dipped into the riverbed, a floor of grooved mud and spikes of sharp stone. The pickup shook its way across. The slowed, but routine, crossing was a very different passage in the rains. Then the calm shallows and the curves of the river often hid flash floods. Their only warning was the sound of roaring water speeding in, a herald too late for many a vehicle before it and its occupants were swept away.

When finally they reached Makindu, they bounced off the road onto a worse track, passing the Temple. They sent word to the watchman to come and meet them there, and then drove on to the nearby Indian *duka* just behind the station.

The priest got out arthritically, and stretched. They moved out of the sun and, entering the dark shop, leaned gratefully against the low bulk of the wooden counter. The *dukawalla* welcomed the new faces, glad to exercise his tongue of birth after an enforced abstinence of a few days. The priest turned in benign fashion to the four, took out a shilling and invited them to have a soft drink. They all sought something cooling. But no ice had been delivered that week to Makindu, and they contented themselves with sharing tepid bottles already reheated by the day.

The priest, Sardar Dalip Singh, then led them to the Temple. This was a small shed-like structure, of mid-twenties vintage, still corrugated iron roof and sides, the faded paint a borrowed PWD plum, the uniform of minor buildings in the Colony. There the caretaker was waiting for them. He fumbled for the keys and, though not an old man, applied a shaking hand to the lock. It was a while before he was able to take it off. They all entered. The thin cement floor had eroded in parts to reveal the earth beneath.

There was silence. The visitors all looked at Mutua. But he said nothing. Finally, in a quiet voice, the Sardar said to Mutua, 'Tell us what you told them in Nairobi.' Still there was silence. 'Tell us what you saw.'

Slowly Mutua pointed to a spot high on the bare wall. His hand still raised, he waited. Finally he began very softly. 'There. I came in last month. It was afternoon. I swept everything. I always sweep everything,' he said. 'You can see.' The Sardar nodded. Again there was a pause. 'I swept. When I looked up,' he raised his eyes to the spot, 'I saw a man on a horse. A man like you people. He was looking at me.'

Nobody said anything. Mutua continued, 'Then I could not see him anymore. I did not know what...I wondered...So I quickly locked up and went home. I did not tell my wife. I did not say anything to others. People would think... Last week when I was cleaning, I clean every week but I always pass here every day, to see that everything is alright, you can ask anybody...' The Sardar patiently waved him on.

'I saw him again, the man on the horse. He had a turban like you people, and a white beard like yours. It was a white horse. This time I looked and looked at him. I could see him for a very long time. The man pointed at your Book there.' Mutua stretched out an arm. 'Then he left.'

Again there was silence. The Swahili words fell on the four uncertain faces. Mutua started again, 'I thought I should tell you people in Nairobi.

About this. What I had seen. Because I had seen him twice. So I took the OTC bus to you. To Nairobi.

'What was this? I did not know. You people might know. So I came to Nairobi.'

The Sardar said softly, 'What happened in Nairobi?'

'I told them. I told them what I am telling you. Ask them. You know them. While I was speaking to them, I saw a picture in their office. It was of the man on the horse who I had seen. I told them that is the man I have seen. They asked me lots of questions, but that is what I had seen. The man in the picture. I told them that.'

No one spoke. The Sardar bent down and out of a bag of coarse cloth took out three framed representations. The first was of a grave man with a beard holding up his palm in a gesture of peace. The next was of a man on a horse, the face looking into the distance, a patch on one eye, a sword in the raised hand. The third was also of a man on a horse with a sword, gazing to his left. In the small dim room, the four stared dumbly at the familiar oleographs.

Before the Sardar could say anything, Mutua, who had been watching him intently, went to the bench and, touching the third frame, said, 'This one. There.' They all looked up into the empty air. 'I saw *him*. There.' He lifted the frame and kept looking at it. No one spoke. The four looked on mutely.

The Sardar began a short prayer almost to himself. His voice droned for a while. Mutua remained with the portrait in his hands. The faces of the four looked on.

At last the Sardar said, 'Come.' They all went out, the intense sunlight bringing them back sharply to the present. The four started whispering amongst themselves. The Sardar took Mutua to one side and began questioning him at length. They talked for a long time, going in and out of the temple, while the four finally attended to the bits of repair and maintenance they had been sent for.

By the early afternoon, they had already started back on the slow drive to Nairobi. In the pickup the four did not stop talking. This time they did not notice the vehicles that passed them or which they overtook. They were oblivious too of the dust and of the smarting heat. Dazzled by what they had heard, they exchanged at last the astonishment they had shared there. Charn—his name signified the feet of God—said, 'It must be true. It *is* true.' The elder two nodded sagely. Even in Nairobi, the temple committee has said so. Everyone is saying it. At one point, the inarticulate Sabjit leaned out of his shyness, 'It was Gobind Singh. The Tenth Guru.' The others looked at him briefly, then carried on talking amongst themselves. Finally they were saying the same things over and over again, their small store of words unable to carry their wonder further. They continued thus for over four hours as they drove home.

Perhaps that faraway Punjab *had* claimed this arid corner. Perhaps it was this arid spot that had claimed these labourers. Perhaps this land, in mute requite, had given just this *one* of its jealously guarded acres to those who, working it so well in wood and metal, had come to find it hard to leave. Otherwise, what was a handsome turbaned soldier on a white horse doing here in Ukambani?

ACKNOWLEDGEMENTS

My love and gratitude first to Villoo Nowrojee, who, as
before, edited many drafts of these stories into what
we remember living.

To Eric Ng'maryo, writer, critic, counsellor, hopelessly
inadequate thanks for his large input as all three.

More thanks:
To Harmesh Mahan and to Mzee Balubhai Sarvaiya,
scholar, for wisdom about our past.

To Hedda and Hermann Steyn for a sanctuary of
tranquillity to complete the book to publication.

To Zarin Nowrojee, apprentice Reader, apprentice
writer, many thanks.

The story 'East Africans' is dedicated with gratitude to
Prof. Yash Pal Ghai.

To Ciira Hirst and Edward Miller, my thanks and
admiration remain for advice and the painstaking
search always for rightness and the finest
craftsmanship.

P.N.

Printed in Great Britain
by Amazon

33742477R00081